Andrew Beauchamp

HALF·A·BUTTON

HALF·A·BUTTON

Lyn Littlefield Hoopes

Pictures by Trish Parcell Watts

A Charlotte Zolotow Book

HARPER & ROW, PUBLISHERS

Half a Button
Text copyright © 1989 by Lyn Littlefield Hoopes
Illustrations copyright © 1989 by Trish Parcell Watts
All rights reserved. No part of this book may be
used or reproduced in any manner whatsoever without
written permission except in the case of brief quotations
embodied in critical articles and reviews. Printed in
the U.S.A. For information address
Harper & Row Junior Books, 10 East 53rd Street,
New York, N.Y. 10022. Published simultaneously in
Canada by Fitzhenry & Whiteside Limited, Toronto.
Typography by Trish Parcell Watts
10 9 8 7 6 5 4 3 2 1
First Edition

Library of Congress Cataloging-in-Publication Data
Hoopes, Lyn Littlefield.
  Half a button / by Lyn Littlefield Hoopes ; illustrated by Trish Parcell
Watts.—1st ed.
      p.   cm.
  "A Charlotte Zolotow book."
  Summary: William and his parents go by sailboat to visit Grampa,
spending a happy day which William can remember long after, whenever
he looks at the half button his grandfather finds and gives him.
  ISBN 0-06-024017-2 : $
  ISBN 0-06-024018-0 (lib. bdg.) : $
  [1. Grandfathers—Fiction.]   I. Parcell, Trish ill.   II. Title.
PZ7.H7703Ha1 1989   87-24949
[E]—dc19   CIP
                                                            AC

For David, with love
L.L.H.

For my William and
in memory of his Grandpa
T.P.W.

William was sailing,
William, his mother and father,
   out through the islands,
from their house
   to Grampa's.

At last they came to Grampa's cove,
   and right to the dock.

William ran first up the blackberry path.

The bees were buzzing in the blackberries,
so he ran fast,
and there was Grampa
at the top of the path,
snipping snapdragons.

"Grampa," shouted William, "surprise!"

Grampa lifted him up
and up, up, slowly, slowly,
then suddenly William was spinning round
high round Grampa's head,
and Grampa said, "Wherever did you come from?"

"The sea!" William shouted.
   Grampa laughed,
his big hugging laugh,
and set William down
among the snapdragons.

One snapdragon was buzzing,
   the whole flower humming,
and buzzing, buzzing.
Gently, Grampa lifted the snap petal,
   and out buzzed a bee,
buzz buzzzzzzzing.

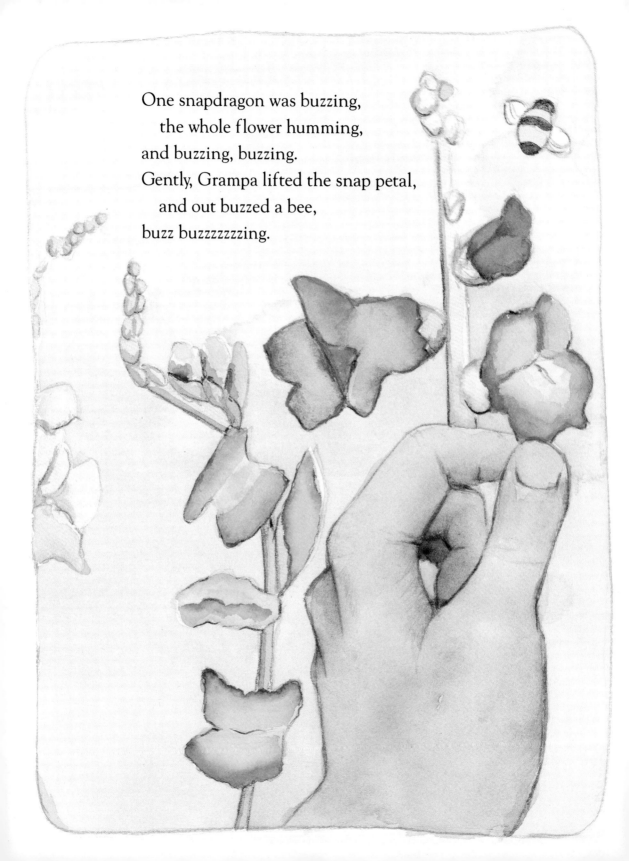

"Surprise!" whispered Grampa.
Then he unzipped William's life jacket,
and snipped the snapdragon for him,
the snapdragon that trapped the bee.

They went together into the old barn,
    out of the wind,
        into the quiet.
There were Grampa's easels and all his paints,
and in the sun shining by the old tub,
William saw Grampa's red bicycle.

"Let's take a ride," whispered William,
    and they went, waving,
past William's mother and father
    tying the boat.

William rode on the crossbar
      and shifted,
down on the up hills,
      up on the down,
and Grampa pedaled round,
      round and round.

The sun flashed tiger stripes
      over the road,
and they slipped through
      dark shade and bright light,
Grampa's wheels popping stones,
leaving their snake trail
      deep in soft dirt,
winding down,
      down to the end of the road.

At the end of the road is the sea.

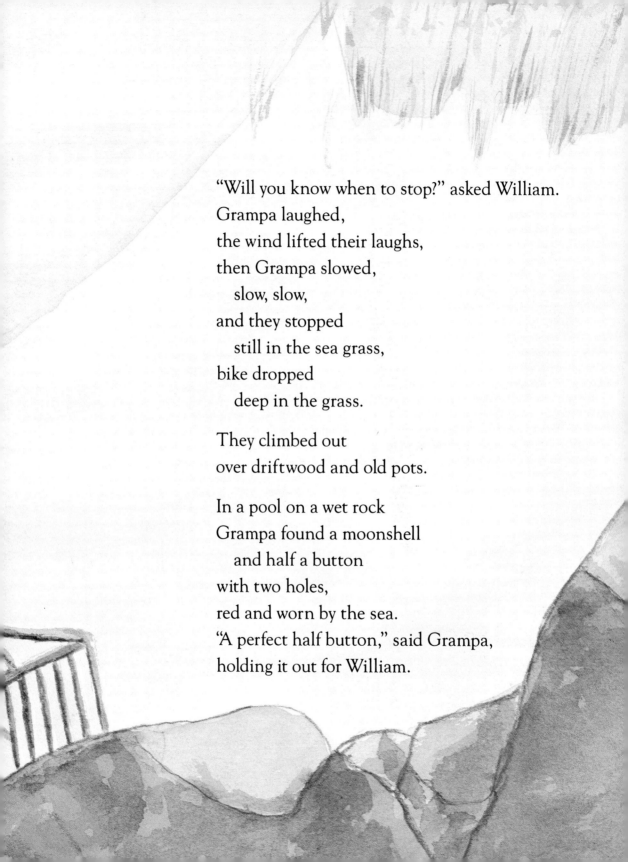

"Will you know when to stop?" asked William.
Grampa laughed,
the wind lifted their laughs,
then Grampa slowed,
    slow, slow,
and they stopped
    still in the sea grass,
bike dropped
    deep in the grass.

They climbed out
over driftwood and old pots.

In a pool on a wet rock
Grampa found a moonshell
    and half a button
with two holes,
red and worn by the sea.
"A perfect half button," said Grampa,
holding it out for William.

William took the button
and held it in his pocket,
all the way home,
up the long hill to Grampa's barn,
where William's mother and father
were waiting.

They had lunch on the rock
by the old barn,
cucumbers from Grampa's garden,
and the wind blew in from the sea,
flapping the soft cloth chairs,
banging the screen door wide.
William's mother and father
lay back in the sun.

William put his head on Grampa's knees
and felt the sea rocking inside him,
    rocking,
and the waves washing,
and the sun heating
    the rock.

He slept.

Then he heard Grampa's boots
soft through the grass,
felt Grampa's shoulder
under his cheek,
Grampa quietly walking,
carrying him down the blackberry path.

Already it was time to go.

Everyone was on the dock,
getting ready,
and Grampa was holding William's hand.

Soon they had everything.

They pushed away
and a little puff filled
their sails, scooting them along
out of the cove.

William looked back at Grampa.

First there was just a little water
between them,
then the water grew and grew
and Grampa stayed there
on the dock, watching.

He waved
and William waved back.

William waved,
and Grampa waved back.

William's mother and father were busy sailing,
but William was watching Grampa
and he knew Grampa was watching him.

Soon they sailed past the point.
William could not see Grampa now,
but he knew he was still
on the dock, there
with the little puffs
blowing round in the cove.

William felt in his pocket
for the half button.

He pulled it out,
and he and his mother and father
sailed on, round the farthest point,
and on,
away from the little cove
and Grampa.

William sat low, out of the wind,
and held the button.
A perfect half button
    with two holes,
red and worn by the sea.